CUL DE SAC TALES II

Margaret Holbrook

This book is dedicated to

Cody, Charlie, Archie and Sophie,
whose names feature in this book.

Without my great nephews and niece
where would Sid have found his
inspiration?

With love to them all.

ABOUT THIS BOOK...

This is the second book of cul de sac tales. There may or may not be another. I wasn't sure there would be a second but eventually Rita got her way. As in the past, Rita comes to the fore when it concerns the good folk of the cul de sac and par for the course, Sid says very little, but then, he doesn't have to.

M.H.

Pronounce Boughden, Bowden, as in bow and arrow.

Also by Margaret Holbrook

Watching and other Stories
Short stories, fiction
Cul de sac Tales
Humour, fiction
Picking the Bones
A collection of tales in the folk tradition
About Us...
Romance, fiction
Broken Ties
Family saga, fiction

Hobby Horses Will Dance, *Poetry*
Not Exactly Life, *Poetry*
Over By Christmas, *Poetry/Short Prose*
WWl theme

Margaret's novel
Remember When You Loved Me
will be published in 2020

THE CUL DE SAC

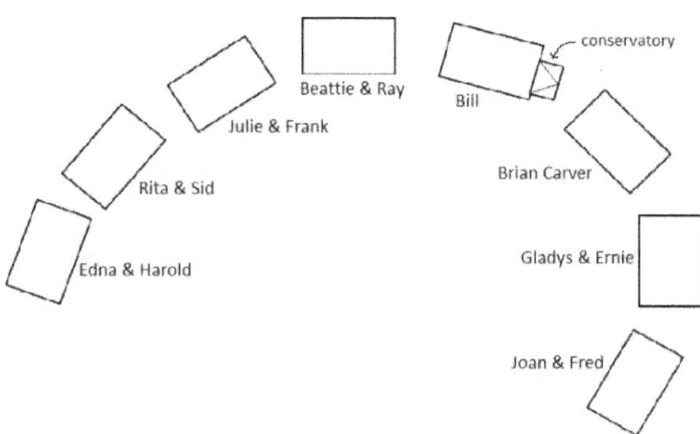

CONTENTS

CATCHING UP

Well, a lot's happened since we last met. Another Royal Wedding, Brexit debate; (we won't go into that. I think it's for the best) and a new Royal Prince, Prince Louis, a brother for Charlotte and George. As you can imagine things on the cul de sac have been pretty hectic. The bunting, red, white and blue of course, has been flying high and lots of quiche and sandwiches and dainty cakes and scones have been consumed. When, or if Brexit happens, I know we'll have a celebration, but no one will mention the politics of it. We get on too well for that and besides we do want a party atmosphere.

On the cul de sac nothing has changed re residents but there have been one or two changes re groups. We now knit and natter. Mostly, but not always it's the ladies but sometimes Bill joins in with us, now who'd have thought that? I suppose it's his army training coming to the fore, now don't ask me why but I think, well I'm pretty certain that they knit and sew in the army although you mustn't take it as gospel. And well, I'm not divulging any state secrets when I tell you *that man can certainly turn a heel.*

We ladies, Edna, Julie, Joan, Beattie and I mainly chat but when we do knit it's mainly squares. We stitch them together to make bed covers and then donate them to the local hospital for the children's ward. They seem to appreciate our efforts, so we feel we're giving something back.

Primrose, Brian's wife has got us active again, although I'm pleased to say it's not in the pool. It's Zumba. We all enjoy it immensely and Primrose helps us through our paces at the local church hall, St Jude's. We meet on a Friday night at seven o' clock and we know that it's doing us good; we can tell by the way we ache afterwards. Anyway, as soon as Primrose can get it organised, we're off on a trip to a local stately home. Primrose has organised that for us. She's ever so good. Nothing is too much trouble. I think Brian landed on his feet with Primrose. We all think she's wonderful.

The trip will include afternoon tea. That was the clincher, really, – afternoon tea, who can resist? We'll be picked up from the cul de sac and brought back home at tea-time, around six-ish.

Harold and Ray aren't coming but they're going to do us an evening meal. Knowing what the weather's been like so far and what Harold's like it will probably be a barbecue. I can't wait.   Primrose will have planned the trip with military precision. She is almost like Bill in her aptitude for planning and making arrangements. She said that she was hoping that the weather wouldn't be too hot for us and had chosen term-time so there would be fewer families. Not that we on the cul de sac are anti young children, we just like a quieter life now we're all of a certain age. Indeed, some of us are grandparents and do childminding duties when required but it's not something we aspire to. You see, we're retired. We like our own free time. And well, just between you and me, Sid and I don't go in for it at all. Our son Nicholas and his wife Trish haven't produced yet. They've been married long enough but we don't like to ask, well it's not the done thing, is it?

Anyway, Primrose said she'd organise the whole thing. It was first mentioned at the cul de sac committee meeting at Bill's a couple of months ago and was carried by an over-whelming majority. So, the upshot is we're off to Boughden's Hall in a small coach. It's about twelve miles from us, so not an exhaustive journey and of course it means a full day at the hall. The family, apparently, still live there so we might just catch a glimpse of them if we're lucky. They have an apartment in one of the wings, Primrose said.

SID CONSIDERS MEN IN SHEDS

Sid's decided to join Men in Sheds, well not join exactly, not yet, but go along and have a look; see what it's all about and then mull it over. He mulls things over a lot does Sid. He doesn't say much but he does a lot of mulling. I think that when he goes, he's hoping to get Brian and Bill to go along, for moral support; well that's what he said.

Bill is still keeping us all busy, on our toes. He's upped the cul de sac committee meetings to every other week, or shall we say once a fortnight, … I thought I'd just drop fortnight in there, you see Bill says it's in danger of becoming *archaic,* like *sennight.* He says it's a case of use it or lose it so he's advised us to drop the word into conversation wherever we possibly can. It's not that we aren't progressive on the cul de sac, we are, but all the same, Bill says we must preserve some of our 'older' English language. He's full of such knowledge, Bill, and we're all very pleased that he's our cul de sac committee leader.

Anyway, where was I? Men in Sheds, yes. I think it'll be a good idea if Sid takes it on because come the wintertime there won't be much to do in the garden and really that's Sid's only pastime, apart from reading the odd book about World War Two. I've told him he could go on Mastermind with all the knowledge he has stored away on that particular subject. So, Men in Sheds would be a good diversion. Something to keep him occupied. I have tried in the past to get Sid interested in volunteering at the charity shop with me but he said that he wasn't quite sure that it was 'his thing'. I'd never known that Sid had a thing, but never mind about that, anyway the thing is Sid's popped round now to catch up with Brian and Bill, to see what they make of it and take it from there. Sid has one or two details already; he knows they meet on Wednesday morning between 9.30a.m. and 12 noon at the church hall and it's only about a five-minute walk so couldn't be better placed really. If you don't know what they do, this particular group, so Sid says, meet up on Wednesday morning and make bird boxes and bird tables, storage boxes, wooden signs, well you get the idea; it's anything made from wood really, and they drink a lot of tea which'll suit Sid down to the ground. I'll excuse him for drinking tea in the morning. It's one day a week after all and he won't be on cul de sac premises. I'd better go and see where he is actually. He'd only gone to check his shed. He's gone very quiet, and that's not unusual, but even so.

He's still outside checking his shed. He'll only be another minute or so he says. I honestly don't know what all the fuss about the shed is. It looks perfectly fine to me, but then, I'm a woman and have totally no idea what is going on in Sid's head half the time. I've given him a nudge, as it were. Brian and Bill might be off and doing something else by the time he gets round to making a move. Oh, here he is. He's just heading off up the path. I can see him from the kitchen window. He must be on his way, well thank goodness for that.

I've decided that while Sid's out of the way I'll sort out one or two cupboards. I can take anything we no longer need over to the charity shop next time I'm in. It's surprising how much comes through the charity shop door and how much goes out but we volunteers all know it's in   a   good   cause.
Joan is calling round to assist. I've recruited her via the landline. I just gave her a quick call and I know a mobile phone has its uses but when I can I like to use the landline. And if I'm in the house I prefer it. If I'm not mobile, then neither's my phone! There goes the doorbell. I expect that'll be Joan.
'Joan, hello, come in. I'll take your

coat. All set for an hour's sorting?'

'Of course, as ever. Have you got everything in lots for me?

'Some. There's a box of ornaments and some of my last season's skirts but I've got to sort out Sid's shirts yet.'

'Ok, you do the shirts and bring them in here and I'll sort what there is here already. Sound like a plan?'

'A good one,' I said.

Joan and I spent a full hour sorting and everything charity shop found its way into the box. Joan wasn't sure about a couple of my skirts and one of Sid's shirts, a Hawaiian design, it was a summer one, obviously. I think he'd got it for one of Bill's famous summer barbecues. Probably only worn it the once. Anyway, my skirt and Sid's shirt went back to the wardrobe. 'Sid's gone to meet up with Brian and Bill to see about going to Men in Sheds. Would Fred be interested? Sid'll have all the details when he comes back.'

Joan and I were having tea and a piece of lemon cake when Sid appeared, (the time had gone past mid-day). Sid seemed quite flustered and I wondered what could have affected him so much. Truth be told, I was worried.

'Are you all right, Sid? You look rather florid for a Wednesday,' I said.

'We've walked back rather briskly and I know it's only a short walk from the church to here but Rita, let me tell you, I'm glad I'm back.'

'You don't look well to me', Joan said. I gave her a look that showed my disdain. That comment wouldn't make anyone feel better. I let Sid go and have a lie down, said that I'd check on him later to see how he was. When I re-joined Joan she said, 'I don't like the look of your Sid.'   'Well Fred's no oil painting either,' I said, then I laughed quietly. 'We've known each other a long time Joan, you know I'm only joking. And I'll check on Sid in a little while. He'll probably be as right as rain after a sleep.'

Joan didn't stay much longer, which was probably a good idea the way things were. I thanked her for all her help and promised to give her a Sid update later that evening.

'How are you now?' I asked Sid when I went to check on him. To be honest Joan's remarks were pretty accurate. Sid didn't look well at all.

'Not good, Rita. I feel all out of sorts,' Sid replied.

'Perhaps I should get the doctor to pop round or make you an appointment at the surgery.'

'If you wouldn't mind, Rita.' That was when I knew it was serious. I phoned Doctor Gill.

'Well Sid, what have you been up to? Not doing too much in the garden. It looks very nice, as usual.'

'No, doctor, just making my way home from the church hall. I'd gone with Brian and Bill, our neighbours, to check out Men in Sheds.'

'Mmm. Anything else? That's it?'

'That's it. We walked back rather quickly but you know it's not that far from here, St. Jude's.'

'No. It shouldn't really have caused too much of a problem. I'll just check your blood pressure. You look a little flushed. Have you had any difficulty breathing, any shortness of breath or dizziness?'

At that point I left Doctor Gill and Sid to get on with the examination/consultation. They could always get me if they needed me and I felt there was nothing I could add to the scenario. What I'd heard was just exactly how Sid had told me it had happened.

It seemed like an age before Doctor Gill left, but thankfully all's well, really. Sid's got slightly raised blood pressure. Doctor said if things didn't improve there was no question but to get in touch with the surgery and someone would come out but I'm so relieved, it's good to know you've got someone there even if they don't say much. Doctor Gill also left a pamphlet. It seems Sid ought to make some lifestyle changes. They could lower his risk of a heart attack in the future. I told Sid I'd do some of the things as well. I think it's better not to do things alone. It's better if you have moral support. We chatted about it, only briefly, as I didn't want to tire Sid too much but cutting down on salt and caffeine and being more active, well those are the things I thought I could do with Sid, and another plus for me was that it might help me in the weight-watching department. Doctor Gill also mentioned that Sid should make an appointment to see the practice nurse to have his blood pressure checked on a regular basis, just to make sure everything's ok. I'll sort that out for him. I really wanted to know about Men in Sheds but that would keep until morning. I was fit to burst not knowing what had happened but well, when you've got a sick husband, their needs must come first.

Sid was much better the following morning and looked more like his perky self, well, perky for Sid, and I told him so. I told him that until I'd done some shopping and changed our usual brand of coffee for decaff, that morning coffee was a 'no, no', as per the doctor's instructions.

I offered Sid breakfast in bed, (only available to menfolk if they're poorly, of course; otherwise, they should come down for breakfast) I read that somewhere. It's etiquette and I do like to keep up standards, well, after all, we are in a cul de sac, but Sid, being Sid, he said that he'd prefer to come down.

I was just in the kitchen making a pot of tea when the doorbell rang. It was Bill. He'd popped round to see how Sid was. Now considering that Bill has no woman to chivvy him along I thought how good it was of him to call. I asked him in, of course, and said that Sid would be down in a minute or two if he'd like to wait. He did. And when Sid joined us, I could see that he was pleased Bill had called round. I stayed out of the way while they were chatting, just provided tea and cake for Bill and a bowl of muesli for Sid. I was starting as I meant to go on. It seemed to go down well and I must say that Sid was a lot brighter after Bill's visit.

'Any news of Men in Sheds?' I asked when Bill had left.

'Of course. We're all going next week.'

'You'll be like the three musketeers,' I said, and smiled.

'No Rita. You've misunderstood. We're all going. All the men in the cul de sac. Bill and Brian asked around yesterday afternoon. Harold, Frank, Ray, Ernie and Fred. It's all of us. Every single one,' and he laughed. 'I know we'll all get a lot from it. I'm pleased Bill and Brian asked the others. And you ladies, well on a Wednesday morning now you can do whatever you like. You'll have some free time away from us men and our testosterone'.

I didn't know what to say to that. I don't think there was much I could say. I went off to make a Victoria Sponge while Sid's hormones calmed down. I thought it was for the best. Especially as how he was fixed at the moment.

HARRY, MEGHAN AND PRIMROSE

Naturally we were all thrilled to have another Royal Event on the cul de sac, not because we're all Royalists but you may have guessed that we cul de sac-ers love a party and a Royal Wedding is as good an excuse as any.

Julie played a major part in the organisation along with Primrose and Gladys. They're really our 'ideas' people. And we oldies don't mind that either. It takes young folk to add to the cul de sac zing and that's something we don't want to lose; as Bill pointed out at a recent cul de sac committee meeting. We all agreed with him of course, I mean we don't want to lose it, do we?

The Royal Wedding event was marvellous. I know Bill had the actual proceedings on the TV in his conservatory but we were just pleased to have a 'do'. I can't actually remember anyone going through to the conservatory to watch, not for long, anyway, but that's another story.

Anyway, during the proceedings Primrose came over to me. 'Rita, I need to talk to someone. It's of a personal nature and as you used to do the agony aunt thing in the charity shop, I wondered would you be a friendly ear?' I was slightly taken aback and I think it might have shown on my face.

'Rita, don't worry. There's no need to be alarmed. It's not too personal. It's friendly advice I need, that's all.'

'Oh, I see. Well, we can't really talk here, not during our event. Why not come round and see me when you're free. A morning would be best for me but fit something in with your work and I'll make sure I'm free. Any morning bar Tuesday. Now don't worry Primrose. Nothing's ever as bleak as it looks.'

'I think it is, sometimes,' she replied.

An arrangement was made for the following Monday, 10.15a.m. Primrose had a late start that morning and it suited her. She said it wouldn't take long. And I could get Sid out in the garden. If he just did small gardening tasks and not for too long, he should be all right. The nurse had given him a clean bill of health re blood pressure, and we were sticking to our healthy living programme. I had coffee ready for when Primrose arrived and some freshly baked scones.

'You shouldn't have gone to so much trouble Rita.'

'It isn't any trouble and besides you know we always do things properly in the cul de sac.'

Primrose smiled, 'Yes,' she said. She sat down while I poured the tea. I could feel that she was watching me and it made me think that what she wanted to discuss might, after all, be serious. I put the teapot down on its tray and looked at   her. 'Well, what is it, Primrose? You look quite concerned.'

'It's Brian.'

'Brian?'

'Yes'.

'What's the problem with Brian. He seems very taken with Men in Sheds, or so Sid says, well they all are actually, taken with it I mean. It's a proper retreat for them.'

'Oh, it's nothing to do with Men in Sheds, that's fine and he does look forward to his Wednesday mornings. In fact, in general, apart from one thing he's fine.'

'I see,' I said, but I didn't really. 'Carry on Primrose. You'd better get to the point and then perhaps I can assist.'

'Yes. I'm sorry but you see Brian, he's not well. Not well at all. I think he might only have a short time left and I would be grateful if you wouldn't let this go any further Rita. No one else must know.'

'You can rely on me,' I said, 'but what's the problem, what is it that makes you so sure he hasn't long left. I mean to be honest Primrose it's quite a lot to take in. Brian always seems so perky.'   There was a pause before Primrose continued. 'He is, but I think he's doing it for me really, putting on a brave face.'

'I suppose that's men all over. Always trying to protect us.'

'I suppose it is. And with Brian it's quite complicated. He's always had a heart condition, well for a number of years and he's managed very well. In fact, he's remarkable, I think you'd agree with that.'

I nodded in response and Primrose continued. 'Recently he's had to have his medication increased. It's a worry. These last few years with Brian, well, since we married, have been the happiest of my life and Rita, it's really affecting me. I can't imagine how I'd cope without Brian. I feel as though there's nothing to look forward to anymore. I feel as though I'm just waiting while Brian becomes more ill and then dies.'

Primrose sighed and I looked at her. 'Don't let it spoil your life together, Primrose. Doing that would only make things all the more difficult for Brian and you wouldn't want that, would you?'

'No, of course I wouldn't but what can I do?'

'Are you sure it's as serious as you say, you know doctors sometimes get things wrong.'

'Yes, it is serious. Brian and I have talked

about it and of course I'll be provided for but I can't bear the thought of him not being there. It's just too much.'

'I understand that. Where is Brian now? Will he mind you talking to me?'

'No. I told him exactly what I was going to do.'

'That's all right then. I think Primrose, that all you can do in this situation is to carry on as if there's nothing changed; for the time being anyway and when you can you make sure that you spend as much time together as you can. Do the things that you both enjoy. The things that brought you both together. I remember when we first met you, Primrose. We'd all been concerned over Brian's welfare and his garden. The safari was imminent. The men put a garden rota together to do Brian's Garden and make sure it met the standard for the safari. Then the day of the event Brian comes back and introduces you as his wife. He surprised us all that day, I must say.'

Primrose laughed. 'Yes, I think some folk thought I was some sort of scarlet woman; after Brian for his house and money but it, I, well it is a love match you know. We both felt the same way. Brian gives me a reason to live.'

'You are the ideal couple, and you Primrose, well you took to the cul de sac like a natural. We wouldn't have done half the things we have without you.'

'Thank you for saying that, Rita. It's kind of you.'

'It's the truth.'

'And Rita, you've helped me clear things in my head. Get things a little more straight. It's always good to have someone to confide in.'

'Pleased to be of help,' I said, and I was. Primrose and I sat for a few more minutes and then I could hear Sid moving about in the kitchen. He came into the lounge, 'Hello,' he said, 'what's this, a secret tea party?'

'No, nothing like that,' I said. Primrose stood up. 'I'd better be getting back. Brian will be wondering where I've got to.'

'Don't rush off,' Sid said, 'not on my account.'

'No Sid, it's fine. I must get on my way. I'm working later this morning.'

AT BOUGHDEN HALL

It was a beautiful May morning, (last week of) when we all set off for Boughden Hall.

The coach arrived promptly at 10.45a.m. as arranged by Primrose. We were all on and away before eleven. It was only £5 each and that included entrance to the hall. I don't know how Primrose manages it, I really don't. It was only a short journey and the traffic wasn't bad, (we were out of the rush-hour, as Primrose pointed out) so we were ready for our morning coffee in the hall's small but immaculate café. It was lovely. The windows were floor to ceiling and overlooked the walled kitchen garden. It was a picture. And also, a biggy this, there was waitress service, wonderful. We waited to be seated and then it was coffee all round.

Primrose had booked us on one of the timed tours of the hall to ensure that we made the most of what was on offer. You find that, don't you, well I do, that if you go somewhere and wander through the rooms you can look but not really take note. If there's someone there to guide you, you get so much more out of it. Of course, I suppose it's each to their own; some people will be quite happy to go through each of the rooms as fast as they can, just to say they've done it. As if it's a tick box list.

Our tour was at 12.45p.m., so plenty of

time to linger over our coffee before we had to be at the meeting point for tours that was situated just outside the main entrance to the hall. Primrose had booked us all into the Old Forge restaurant, (adjacent to the café) for afternoon tea at 3.30p.m. That was an extra charge of £10 each but everyone in the cul de sac agreed it was a very competitive price. I mean, £15 for everything, afternoon tea, coffee, and a tour of the hall plus coach hire. A bargain.

At 12.40p.m. we were all waiting at the appointed place for our tour of the hall. At 12.42p.m. our guide arrived. She looked very smart and sported a name badge. 'J. Smart'. I nudged Sid, 'She suits her name,' I whispered, and smiled. Sid didn't take me on.   At 12.44p.m. J. Smart spoke. 'Good afternoon everyone. My name is Justine Smart and I'm your guide for your tour of Boughden Hall this afternoon. We'll begin here in The Great Hall and continue through and up the stairs to the first floor before going down the stairs at the opposite side of the hall before we finally end up back here, where we started; The Great Hall. The whole tour will take about one hour. Please ask any questions as we go through the house and please in the event of an alarm going off it is not a drill, so do keep together and follow me. I will lead us all safely to the nearest fire exit. Also, there are no lifts in the hall. There are stairs and some of them are narrow and quite steep. Please be careful. If you are going to find the stairs a problem, let me know and I will contact a colleague to bring you back to this point after the tour of the ground floor is complete. Finally, the Boughden family are in residence today. Do not speak to them unless, and I must stress this point, unless they speak to you first. And then we were off. Primrose, as group leader of our party was at the front with Justine. I stayed with Joan and Fred and Sid stayed back to keep an eye on everybody. He was our back-marker, making sure we didn't lose anyone. Also, it suited Sid, as after his little health scare, being at the back meant he could go at his own pace. He didn't have to walk so fast. So, it suited him down to the ground and, I think, it gave him a bit of authority, which, secretly, I think he quite enjoyed. I remarked to Joan that Justine was rather like our very own Dame Joan.

'Joan Sutherland. How do you know, does she sing?'

'No, not that Dame Joan. The other one, Joan Bakewell,' I said.

'Oh,' Joan replied, 'I'm sorry. I can't see the likeness myself.'

'No, she doesn't look like her. It's her manner.'

'What about her manner?'

'Well, it's authoritative. She won't stand for any nonsense and she knows her facts. She's not your friend but she'd be a good ally, should one be needed. She'd be empathetic to your cause if she supported it.'

'What if she didn't support it,' Joan said.

'Well then you've no chance,' I replied.

Justine gestured for everyone to gather by a beautiful, mullioned window at the opposite end of The Great Hall. 'This room, as you can see is bright and light and this window, if you look carefully at the glass, you will see there are some initials scratched onto it, also some symbols. We think that these date from when the house was built in the late 16th century. Also note the doorway opposite. That is the main doorway. It looks from the outside like a large, high entrance built to impress, but it is not. Anyone entering from the outside could only come through into The Great Hall one at a time, and they could not carry swords. The door on this side as you can see is low and narrow. It is a 16th century security system. Do have a look at the outside of the door when you look around the grounds later. The next room we will go to is through the door to your left, that takes us to The Lesser Hall.'

We followed Justine. Once we were all inside the room she started speaking again. 'The Lesser Hall was used mainly as a sitting room and the doors from here lead through to the library where we will go next, and the main Dining Hall, which is through the door to your right. The rooms on this side of the house were the first to be built on this site and there is plenty of interest from here on in.'

I loved it. Justine was a marvellous guide. She knew her stuff and I enjoyed history. What a good idea from Primrose to get this trip organised. I would of course thank Primrose personally, later. I don't think any of the cul de sac-ers could believe how quiet I was, particularly Sid, but you see I was held rapt by Justine's knowledge of Boughden Hall.

After the tour we headed straight for the Old Forge restaurant for our afternoon tea. Justine had escorted us all across the courtyard, keeping chatting to Primrose as we went on and leaving us all at the restaurant, she bid us farewell. I daresay she had another party waiting for her. I noticed as we made our way to our table that Bill was at the back of the group and he was chatting to Justine. He certainly made her smile whatever it was he was saying. It was only a few minutes of course because he came and sat down virtually at the same time as Sid and when I turned to look Justine was nowhere in sight. I looked knowingly at Joan and Beattie but they just smiled. They hadn't seemed to notice anything, so I kept 'mum'. To say anything at all wouldn't have been right.

The afternoon tea was first class. Finger sandwiches and dainty cakes and scones. What a day it had been. When we had all had sufficient of everything, I raised a vote of thanks to Primrose for organising such a perfect outing. Everyone of course, was with me and Brian raised his glass, 'To my perfect wife, Primrose.' I looked at them both and smiled, then I applauded, 'Come on everyone, let's finish our day in true cul de sac style.' And we did. We had an hour to kill before the coach would be there to pick us up. I went with Sid, Primrose and Brian and Joan and Fred to have a look at the door of the hall from the outside. It was amazing. Then we went into the gift shop to pick up one or two souvenirs. Bill was in there with Edna and Gladys and Ernie. We all seemed to have had the same idea, tea towels and fudge. Well, what better way was there to finish a trip to a truly British house and garden?

I felt pleased that Brian had seemed to have had a good day as well. I was a little surprised that he'd decided to come along truth be told but I think he was sensible in that he restricted his activities. I think Primrose probably had a hand in that.

As we headed back to the rendezvous point for the coach I chatted to Primrose. 'You've organised a super trip today. It has been so enjoyable. I think it will go down in the cul de sac archives as one to remember. Thanks Primrose.'

'I'm just glad everyone got on so well. And Justine, she's up to the mark, isn't she? She certainly knows her stuff. I think we did well to get her as a guide. You can't ask for anyone specific, you just book the tour and see who you end up with.'

'Well we ended up with a star,' I said.

We were soon on the coach and heading homeward. The time had passed all too quickly but as I walked through the door of our bungalow that evening, I felt elated. It must have shown as Sid actually remarked on it. I smiled, 'It's nothing. We've just had such a lovely day together, haven't we?'

Sid smiled. 'We have,' he said. Sid didn't know what I had on my mind and I wasn't going to say anything, not just yet. I went to freshen up and then we joined the others in Bill's conservatory. I couldn't wait to see what delights Harold and Ray had cooked up for us.

ZUMBA

We cul de sac-ers, (ladies only, of course) all enjoyed Zumba class and it was thanks to Primrose that we were Zumba-ing at all.

I did wonder after her recent revelation whether she would carry on but she did. And looking at Primrose as she went through the moves no-one could have guessed at the sorrow she was carrying. She was definitely made of stern stuff. A true inspiration.

Of course, there were some ladies who couldn't join in or those who tried and failed but at least we gave it a go. The younger ones, Primrose and Julie were very good, as was Beattie, for all that she said she was feeling older these days and was 'cutting back'.

I did try some of the more difficult moves and that was how it was for me, difficult. I did stay though. I enjoyed it, as much for the chat as for the Zumba. Joan did try to stay and hoped she would improve with time but unfortunately Joan was one of the Zumba casualties.

Primrose knew the instructor, (I think it was something to do with her work, their paths had crossed) and informed us that he also took Aqua Zumba if we fancied it but after my 'pool problems' with Aqua Fit I told her that it wasn't for me. Most of the other ladies from the cul de sac were with me on this one so we Zumba-ed away for an hour on a Monday evening, 7-8p.m.. It meant we couldn't eat a meal before the class, (we wouldn't have Zumba-ed at all if we had) but we soon got into the habit of going to The Old Duke for a meal afterwards, only something light mind you, but to be honest it was the part of the evening I looked forward to most. As I said I was pleased to see that Primrose still wanted to come along considering Brian's ill health but it was on the proviso that Brian called Sid if he felt even slightly off colour or out of sorts.

Our Zumba instructor was called Cecil. He wasn't at all South American or Latin looking but he *could* Zumba. I don't think Cecil did much for him as a name but it had probably suited him as a baby. Anyway, that's just me but Cecil was very good and he could move and had great flexibility which was something we were all keen to achieve. If you're wondering what exactly we do on a Monday evening, wonder no more. Cecil described it thus at one of our first classes, 'Zumba, is a form of aerobic exercise and a fitness programme based on Latin American dance music. So, ladies, if you fancy having a salsa or merengue and *Strictly* type dance classes seem out of your league this is a do-able option. It's fun and it's more of an hour-long dance party than a fitness workout'.

Cecil wasn't wrong. We actually do have a party. We spend a lot of time laughing, (not too loudly) as Cecil doesn't like it and he reprimands us if we become too boisterous. When I say 'reprimands' it's not as bad as it might seem; he gives us, as he calls it, *the look of the master.* It's more of a directed scowl aimed at whoever has done wrong.

As I said, Julie and Primrose were the best Zumba-ers in the cul de sac but of course it wasn't only us who attended the class. There were around twenty in the whole group and some of them were really very good. Of course, they were probably only in their twenties or thirties but they were excellent and had achieved levels which we were never going to reach. Some of them could bend in places you would never imagine and without causing any problems or visits to A&E.

Cecil said that it didn't matter. That as long as we did our best, we could be pleased with whatever we achieved. We weren't to compare ourselves with others in the class just for the sake of it. He was a very astute man and very likeable. If he had lived in the cul de sac I felt that he would have been an excellent addition to the cul de sac team.

Of the younger ones it was a young woman named Zara who I considered to be the best, but then I'm no expert and I rarely agree with the judges on Strictly Come Dancing, which I watch for fun but with a judge's eye. I think of 'Strictly' as a game of smoked salmon proportions. It's either love or hate. I am of the former opinion whereas Bill, our cul de sac committee leader is of the latter but then he is a man and not, I think, a dancer and with men I often say that it's sometimes difficult to know where you are. Cecil always played nice Latin American music. In a way it took me back to when Sid and I had just married. Latin American music was very popular then, in the early 60s. Mas Que Nada was a particular favourite but with any of the Latin rhythms you can't really go wrong.

At the end of the Zumba class, we warm down. I like that. We stand first and do shaking movements with our arms. Then we sit and rotate our ankles, in both directions, Cecil is insistent on that. It's funny you know; I have one ankle that rotates better than the other. My right ankle rules supreme in the warm down stakes. My left is, well, my left is not very good.   At the end of the warm down we relax. We lie down and close our eyes for two or three minutes. That, Cecil tells us is very important and not to be missed out. *'You must warm down,'* he says. Every week he says it and with great authority. And then we leave – class over – until next week.

As we were leaving this particular evening and saying our goodbyes and ready to make our way home via The Old Duke, Primrose tugged at my arm, gestured to me. 'I can't make the meal tonight,' she whispered, 'I want to get home and make sure Brian's all right. I'm worried. Please Rita, will you make my excuses to the others?'

When we all arrived back on the cul de sac at around 9.30p.m. an ambulance passed us on the way out. There were no sirens but the lights were flashing. I knew everyone else would have seen it so Primrose wouldn't be able to keep her secret any longer. I didn't say anything but went straight in to Sid. I asked if Brian had phoned him. 'No,' he said, 'is something wrong?'

'Probably,' I replied and went straight round to Primrose and Brian's bungalow. I was wondering whether this might have been Primrose's last Zumba.

TUESDAY IN THE CHARITY SHOP

At our next shift at the charity shop Brian and Primrose were on our minds, mine and Joan's and Muriel's, our manageress. Muriel had to be brought up to speed of course and immediately said that she'd help in any way she could. She said that she'd let Sylvia know. Sylvia, you may remember was a volunteer but married Rob from The Tan Lan Fryery and now spent most of her time with her husband, understandably so. And also you might remember that Sylvia, I thought, wasn't quite up to the standards we'd expect for volunteering in the charity shop, well, all that's in the past. I must say that since her marriage she's a changed woman. She's turned into quite a nice person. She's more rounded as an individual. At least I think that's the phrase the younger ones bandy about.

Primrose wasn't at home much. She was at the hospital spending as much time with Brian as she could. And there again, when Brian and Primrose married, there were some of us in the cul de sac, myself included, who wondered whether it was a love match; but as time went on and we all got to know her, we knew that it was right. And now, well there could be no doubt at all. They were made for each other.

Anyway, after Joan and I had a short

chat I checked the racks for my skirts, the ones I'd donated. I was pleased to see they'd all been sold. I know some folk won't donate clothes to local charity shops as they're afraid someone might recognise them and say such as, 'Well, you wouldn't have thought Joyce or whoever was that big, would you?' (I am using the name Joyce as an example. I don't personally know any big Joyces. Anyway, it doesn't bother me if folk think my clothes are big; because someone's buying them and *they* must be of similar proportions. And it's easier than making a journey of a few miles to the next town, (which some folk do) to donate and where probably the folk might say, 'This is Mrs X's donation, the lady from Water Row, (another made up name) she always brings her things here, can't think why. There's a perfectly good charity shop where she lives'.

Anyway, where was I? Yes, all my skirts had sold, good. And that was when Muriel came out of the office. 'Ladies,' she said, 'I've a really good idea but it's down to you two really.'

Joan and I looked at Muriel in amazement. 'What have we done?' I asked.

'Given me an idea for a fund-raiser.'

'And it is …?' Joan asked.

'It is that you two, my best volunteers, give a storytelling session dressed as gypsies, of course; head scarves, large golden earrings, long skirts. We're bound to have something you can borrow from stock for the evening.'

'Why in the evening and why are we dressed as gypsies?' I asked.

'Because,' Muriel continued, 'I'm opening the shop in the evening to get more interest. There will be a supper, provided by The Tan Lan, of course, and why the costume? For atmosphere of course. Who can resist a story from a couple of gypsy ladies?' Muriel smiled as she finished speaking.

'What's it in aid of?' Joan asked. 'We need to know. After all we have supposedly given you the idea.'

'Yes. And what a good idea. I've decided we'll raise funds for the Cooper Ward.'

'That's where Brian is,' I said.

'Yes. I know, and that's why I've decided on this venture. What do you say ladies, are you in?' I suppose you know now what our answer was. I mean, how could we refuse?

You can imagine what it was like as Joan and I walked home. Our heads were in a whirl. We decided we'd get together at Joan's the following morning over coffee and discuss. Meanwhile we'd each spend the evening trying to sort out what stories we could tell for the

Spellbound event at the charity shop in three weeks' time.

Our discussion the next morning was very high octane I can tell you. Before we went further than the basics, however, we decided to let the other cul de sac-ers in on exactly what Muriel envisaged. We did a very quick door to door.

Primrose, although of course distressed by Brian's condition, which, she said, showed very little improvement, thought the *Spellbound* evening an excellent idea.

A few of the ladies promised support and were at once designated to assist The Tan Lan with refreshments, (they would provide cakes and sweet treats.)

The men, of course were at Men in Sheds but we could get to them later and their good ladies would pass on a message in the meantime. The only one we didn't get to was Bill, so we left a note. I left a note for Sid asking him to pop round to Joan and Fred's when he arrived home.

Sid was very keen to take part and to an extent this surprised me. I'd thought of him as being a willing and supportive audience member but this new side of him was quite a revelation. I think it was all to do with Men in

Sheds, (who'd now added extra slots to their meeting times.) I think it had brought him out a little and I must say I was pleased with the changes.

Fred was non-committal. 'He's bound to help in some way,' Joan remarked. 'He always likes to be involved. I daresay he'll be better after he's eaten.'

A few minutes later Bill was at the door. He said he would pop into the shop and have a word with Muriel re helping with arrangements, he was after all that type of person. Joan and I agreed to pave the way with Muriel for him and he seemed to appreciate that, although after he'd left Joan did remark that his mind seemed to be elsewhere.

Back in the lounge Sid surprised me yet again. 'Rita, Joan, I've been thinking what I could do for the event. I'd like to read a monologue if I may. I think I'm settled on The Runcorn Ferry'. It didn't mean a lot to me but I said I was sure it would go down well. One always has to encourage in these situations. Sid smiled and said he'd go back home now and get something to eat. Joan and I carried on with our task in hand. 'Fred will sort himself out', Joan said. 'We'd best carry on with the planning while we're on a roll.'

We soon had our slot virtually planned and we did it all over coffee and as Joan said, 'the optional coffee and walnut cake,' we both indulged. I remarked on the light bright flavour of the walnuts. Joan told me they were Turkish. I wasn't surprised.

We were soon settled on our tales. We would do a version of the 'The Little Match Girl' and a piece local to our area, 'The Lost Boy.' Apparently, (and how much truth there is in this I don't know) a boy in the early 1900s was sent one morning by his father a local landowner, to go with the farm manager to take two horses to market. The farm manager returned but not the boy, who was heir to the farm and the land for miles around. The farm manager denied having any knowledge of what had happened to the boy but the boy's father doubted this. Anyway, long story short, the boy was never seen again. The farm manager hangs himself in a barn some three years later and the landowner dies a broken man, leaving the land and all his property and chattels to the local people for their use and pleasure.

I phoned Muriel and explained Sid would like to read The Runcorn Ferry. Muriel hadn't heard of it but I explained or tried to; 'it's 2d per person per trip.' Muriel was none the wiser. I left it there regarding the monologue and Muriel said that perhaps Sid should be the interval entertainment dressed as a Gypsy King. 'He can borrow anything that's suitable from stock,' she said, 'can he play a violin?'

'It's whether I can get him to wear an earring,' I said. 'He's not what you'd call a modern man.'

'He'll be perfect,' Muriel said, 'anyway, I'd better go now, we've a queue forming at the till. Bye.'

I looked at Joan. What do you think Joan? Muriel wants Sid to be a Gypsy King. Do you think Sid could do it?'

'Gypsy Kings don't need to be modern,' Joan said, 'a Gypsy King of any type would sweep a girl off her feet. Think David Essex. Tell Sid to think David Essex.'

'David Essex had nothing to do with the Runcorn Ferry,' I said.

Joan said I was missing the point. 'I'll speak to Sid when I get home. I'll do my best but I'm not promising anything,' I said.

Joan and I thought we'd end our slot with a song, with Muriel's permission of course, just so we didn't send everyone home miserable.

The night of the event was soon upon us. Sid and some of the other men from Men in Sheds had made a very convincing crystal ball. Don't ask me how. Just believe me when I tell you it worked wonderfully. Wood, is very versatile. And yes, Sid made a very convincing Gypsy King, complete with violin. He can't play of course; it was just used as a prop. He put on an accent, not exactly Runcorn and not exactly anywhere else, either, but the audience were with him from the start. Joan and I also looked quite convincing as gypsies with clothes and accessories from the shop. And on the night, Muriel gave us each a small tambourine. They were festooned with ribbons and we gave them a shake as and when we thought appropriate.

We told our stories with great aplomb. The audience were eating out of our hands. It's only a pity that our singing let us down. Singing acapella over a certain age is not such a good idea. Not without training, anyway. We thought we weren't bad, not too bad. Good enough to get through at any rate but that's where what you hear and what the audience hears comes into question. They applauded us. They laughed with us. They thought our singing had been planned this way. It wasn't. We were doing our best. They thought it was the comedy slot to bring the evening to a close. We felt like crying but cul de sac women are made of stern stuff. We carried on, upping our effort. The audience took us to their hearts. They requested an encore. We accepted graciously. Two outings of Come into The Garden, Maud, was more than enough for anyone.

Muriel said that Bill had helped enormously with the planning and she thanked him for his efforts on the night. He wasn't however on his own at the event. There was a woman on his arm. It was Justine Smart from Boughden Hall.

I had mixed feelings about this. Obviously, I was pleased for Bill but I was hoping my new position as room steward at the hall would not be put in jeopardy; after all, Justine Smart was going to be my boss and I would be starting my new position in two weeks.

I hadn't told anyone, not even Sid, but I had taken an application form on the day of the cul de sac visit to the hall and filled it in and sent it off. I wasn't expecting to get a reply inviting me along to the hall but I had. I decided to keep my news a secret for a day or two longer and then see what Sid made of it. I hoped he would be pleased for me.

After I'd been back to the hall for a short interview. I received another letter. I had passed muster. I was going to be a Boughden Hall volunteer. I still didn't tell anyone. I didn't know how to tell them really. It all was very exciting and yet daunting. I'd have another sleep on it and perhaps make a start by telling Sid in the morning.

Muriel told us she was very pleased with us the next time Joan and I were in on a shift together. She said that the audience had loved the event and thought it was a great way to fundraise. And then Muriel paused slightly before continuing… 'and with the ticket price and the raffle and the generosity of the bucket collection at the end of the evening we raised just shy of £350 for the Cooper Ward at the hospital.'

'How much short?' I asked.

'£2.37 pence.'

'That's not bad. I mean that's really very good,' Joan said.

'It is,' I added.

Muriel continued, 'Of course it will be £350 we present as a cheque to the hospital. I'll make up the small deficit. It's the least I can do after everything you and your fellow cul de sac-ers did on the night.'

'Can we tell them?' I asked, 'about the amount raised?'

'Not just yet,' replied Muriel. 'I'm

meeting up with Primrose this afternoon and I'd like her to know the details first. After that it's open season.'

'I agree entirely,' I said. 'I'm just so pleased about everything that I completely forgot all about fund raising protocol.'

'Mmm,' Joan added, 'and that's not like you at all.'

Muriel went into the office and left us to get on with the work of the charity shop.

Our costumes, freshly laundered and pressed were ready to add to the stock and there were more items ready sorted and priced in the back stock room. It was a never-ending task but raised vital funds, and, to some of our regulars we were a lifeline. A warm place to spend the odd half hour or so, to have a chat, (we had quite a sizeable widowed clientele) and of course catch up on local news and perhaps bag a bargain. We literally had something for everyone.

'I wonder if Brian's feeling a little better as Primrose is spending some time with Muriel this afternoon to talk over the event. It does mean she'll be away from Brian you see and that's so unlike Primrose. She has been so attentive during all of his illness.'

'I don't know', I replied. 'I would imagine Muriel just wants to do things properly. And it will probably only take a short time, perhaps no more than 15-20 minutes, so knowing Primrose, she'll have covered all bases; she's probably arranged for someone else to visit and to sit with Brian while she's away.'

'You're right Rita. I hadn't thought of that.'

We carried on sorting stock and filling the racks and shelves. It was a bit of a slow morning and then Mr. Drummond came in. He wasn't an awkward man but he was someone you'd rather avoid. As we saw him approach Joan and I bobbed down behind the gents' overcoats. It was no use. He'd seen us and pulled the hangers apart to reveal mine and Joan's astonished faces.

'Lost something ladies?' he asked.

'No,' Joan said.

'Yes,' I said.

We had spoken simultaneously, much to the amusement of Mr. Drummond. 'I'll take that as a 'no',' Mr. Drummond said, returning the hangers to their original positions and leaving Joan and me struggling to get upright.

Retired knees are not at their best when they've been in a kneeling position for more than one minute.

I feel I must point out at this juncture that our knees, mine and Joan's, are our own. They have not been provided by the NHS, so we consider ourselves lucky.

When we emerged from behind the coats and were in a standing position Mr. Drummond was standing by the counter.

'Ah ladies, now that I have your attention, I'd like to show you something.' Mr. Drummond withdrew a small bag from his overcoat pocket and placed it on the counter. 'Do I have your attention ladies?'

Joan and I looked at each other and then at Mr. Drummond. 'Yes,' we replied in unison. Mr. Drummond then opened the bag and took from it a small pair of nut-crackers.

'They don't work,' he said, 'I bought them the week before last. I think you'll remember my coming into the shop.'

'I do,' Joan said. 'I dealt with the sale. £1.99, you gave me a five-pound note, put the penny in the collection box you said, and then you took the £3 change and put it into your pocket.'

'Correct,' said Mr. Drummond.

'Well,' I said.

'Well, what?' Mr. Drummond said.

'Well, why are we looking at them

now,' I said.

'They don't work,' Mr. Drummond said.

'Oh,' Joan said, quietly as though not wanting to be heard.

'And I'd like a refund,' Mr. Drummond said.

'Oh, well, we'll have to get Muriel our manageress. She deals with all things of this sort,' Joan said.

'You'll have to get her then,' Mr. Drummond replied.

Joan went to the office. I stayed with Mr. Drummond and his nutcrackers.

To make conversation I said, 'What nuts have you tried them on?'

'Walnuts,' he replied.

'And you couldn't crack any nuts with them, any walnuts, I mean?'

'No. Not a one. I had to resort to a toffee hammer which wasn't much good at all.'

'No. I can imagine.'

'So, you see my predicament. These nutcrackers are not fit for purpose. They've been mis-sold and I would like a refund.'

I turned towards the office and was relieved to see Joan and Muriel approaching.

'Ah. Help is at hand,' I said.

Mr. Drummond smiled, sneeringly. I just decided I didn't really like him. I hoped it wasn't obvious.

'Ah, Mr. Drummond,' Muriel said, 'and how can I help you today?'

'Hasn't she told you?' he said, pointing at Joan.

'Yes, Mr. Drummond, but I'd like to hear the story from you; to make sure we have all the facts.' Mr. Drummond, obviously taken aback obliged Muriel with his story. When he had finished Muriel took the nutcrackers in her hands. 'These nutcrackers, Mr. Drummond, they're strictly ornamental.'

'I wasn't told that when I bought them. Your assistant was remiss. I wouldn't have bought them if I'd known they were merely ornamental.'

'I'm sorry about that Mr. Drummond but if you want a refund, I'll have to try them and unfortunately I haven't any nuts…'

'I have,' Mr. Drummond replied, 'they're in my other pocket.' Mr. Drummond took a small brown paper bag from his coat pocket. He took from it five walnuts, in their shells. 'Here you are,' he said to Muriel.

'Thank you, Mr. Drummond.' And then Muriel placed a nut into the small, wooden cylinder of the nutcracker. Joan and I watched, transfixed. Slowly, Muriel turned the screw piece of the nutcracker down onto the hard shell of the walnut. Then she turned the screw piece again holding the cylinder firmly and exerting pressure on to the nutshell. 'One more turn, I think,' she said. And then we heard it, CRACK!, the shell was broken.

Mr. Drummond looked up from the walnut and into the eyes of Muriel. 'I'm amazed,' Mr. Drummond said, 'really amazed.' And then he smiled. And this time it was a smile. A proper smile. Mr. Drummond gathered the remaining nuts together, putting them back into the brown paper bag and then replacing the bag in his pocket. The nutcracker was replaced likewise into his other pocket. 'Thank you very much for your assistance, ladies. I appreciate your help.' Joan and I smiled. Mr. Drummond exited the shop, on doing so he turned and thanked us again. Muriel looked at us. 'Well, Mr. Drummond is in rather a strange mood, isn't he?' Joan and I had to agree. It rather unsettled us. It was so unlike him to be quite so thankful. He usually ended up leaving the returned goods with us and his 'refund' in the appropriate coins, in his hand. £4.50 was the most Mr. Drummond ever spent in any one transaction, so the refund was always in coins. Muriel returned to the office, Joan and I to stocking and tidying the shelves. We didn't talk much. We were too flabbergasted by what had happened. Sometimes volunteering had a strange, surreal side to it. I would be glad to get home and talk to Sid, not that he'd say much of course but talking to anyone helps, even a listener.

My mind was beginning to drift. I wondered about Sid and what he might be doing. Sometimes, if he thought on, a pot of tea would be ready for my return. I hoped today might be one of those days. In my mind, they were the golden days.

'Rita, Rita,' I was shaken from my thoughts by Joan. 'Are you all right, Rita? You seem a little vague. As though you're somewhere else.'

'Fine thank you Joan. Just thinking.'

'About something nice?'

'Nothing in particular but I was actually wondering whether Sid will have the tea brewed for when I get in.'

'It's nearly time we were off anyway. Only a couple more minutes and we'll be all done.'

As if on cue Muriel came out of the office. 'You may as well be off now. Thank you, ladies.'

Joan and I collected our things and set off out of the shop. As we opened the door to leave, we passed Primrose. She smiled, 'Is Muriel inside?'

'Yes,' I said. 'If you can't see her in the shop just knock on the office door. She'll not be far away'.

JUSTINE TIME

Bill who'd always been a stalwart of the cul de sac community group had cancelled a meeting, the one called for Wednesday evening. He said that something had come up at short notice and could we re-schedule. Well, as the meetings took place in Bill's conservatory there didn't seem much that we could do about it. The meeting was deferred. It was a pity because there was plenty to discuss. The most important item on the agenda was Brian's garden. As you know, we have rotas. We give one another a hand in times of crisis and now it seemed that one of our residents was having a terrible crisis and we weren't able to help, not officially.

Sid said to hold back and not get too hasty galvanising folk into action. He said that Bill would take everything into hand and the meeting was only deferred for a week.

'It's not like Bill to do things like this. He's usually organised and woe betide anyone who gets in his way or doesn't show.'

'Probably got a lot on his mind,' Sid said.

'Haven't we all,' I said, 'but we don't go cancelling arrangements.'

Sid smiled. 'Let it go now love, leave it. I'll go and pour some tea. It's brewed.'

'A golden day,' I said.

Sid didn't reply. I didn't think he

would. Sid brought the tea through to the lounge. I smiled at him, 'Thanks. I'm ready for this.' And I was.

I drank my tea and sat myself back in the chair. I was soon asleep. I don't know how long I nodded off for, but I was wakened by Sid. 'Rita, Rita. It's next door. Julie, she just wants a quick word. Is that ok or shall I tell her you're asleep?

'You'll tell her no such thing. I'll just give my hair a quick brush and I'll be right. Well, don't stand there on ceremony Sid, go and tell Julie to come through. It could be important. Oh, and while you're in that direction you may as well put the kettle on. Julie will be ready for a drink, I'm sure.' Sid looked at me, quizzically but then turned and carried on his way to the door. A couple of minutes later and Julie joined me. 'Sit down Julie. Would you like some tea. The kettle is on.'

'Oh, that would be nice, thank you.'

I went through to the kitchen and carried on where Sid had left off. I glanced through the kitchen window. Sid had gone down to the shed. *Good, he's leaving us to chat. I won't have to worry about him getting underfoot.*

I came back through to the lounge with a tray. 'Sid's in the garden. I spotted him in the shed just now. I don't know what he does out there but it keeps him occupied.'

'They're all the same,' Julie said, and smiled. I poured the tea.

'No cake for me,' Julie said, 'I'm trying to lose a few pounds.'

'Well, I won't bother either,' I said, 'although old habits die hard. I'll move the cake out of the way then it won't be a temptation.'

'Good idea. I'm honestly hoping that Zumba will help me in the weight loss department. I'm trying to get the body beach bikini ready.'

That surprised me. I said nothing and took the cake into the kitchen.

I couldn't help it though and on my return the words just fell from my lips. 'I didn't know you did the two-piece,' I said.

'A woman of mystery, that's me,' Julie replied 'and apparently, it's not just me who has an air of mystery about them. After all, Bill deferred the cul de sac committee meeting.'

'Yes, of course,' I replied, 'and at such short notice.'

Julie leaned forward. 'Do you know why?' she asked.

'No. No one has said anything.'

'It's Justine Smart.'

'Justine?'

'Yes.'

'Oh.'

'Yes. They're walking out. Our Bill and Justine Smart are an item.'

'Oh. Well, we'd better watch how we handle this, Julie. We don't want any gossip starting, not in the cul de sac. It wouldn't be right.'

'No. Of course you're right, but this, our conversation that we're having now, it's not gossip Rita. It's just keeping other committee members up to speed.'

'Other members know?' I asked.

'Of course. I felt it the right and proper thing to do.'

Julie left soon after our conversation but I didn't mention any of what had been said to Sid. I just asked him about Men in Sheds. Apparently, Bill had missed the last two meetings.

I left Sid tidying away the tea things. I had to watch him with the cake. I said I'd put it away. Truth be told, I didn't want him sneaking even a small slice. Not after his earlier health scare. That done, I came and sat down in the lounge. I knew Sid would be alone with the cake even if it was back in the tin but, *but* I didn't want to turn into a helicopter wife, always hovering.

It's for the best in the long run. Men have to have a bit of space.

I was thinking about Bill and Justine but I was also thinking about Brian and Primrose. I hoped things were looking up . And Primrose, Primrose had added to cul de sac life immensely with all her new ideas and activities for us to try. And Zumba wouldn't be the same.

I felt sad and quite helpless and that's not like me at all.

'What's up love?' Sid asked when he came in from the kitchen.

'Not much. Just things. Cul de sac things. It seems as though everything that we know might be set for a change.'

Sid didn't reply but then I don't suppose there was anything that he could have said.

JOAN TO THE RESCUE

I hadn't seen Joan for a day or two but I knew that Julie had been keeping up with everyone so I wasn't bothered by this and I knew that I had rather been keeping myself to myself.

Anyway, there was a knock at my door, (well, rather more a ring of the doorbell) and it was Joan, with a rota. She waved it under my nose when I opened the door.

'All the men are busy being Men in Sheds, so I thought I'd pop round.'

'Come in. I'll pop the kettle on.' I checked my watch, 11.30a.m.. 'Coffee all right for you Joan?'

'Perfect.'

'I'll only be a minute. You sit down and then we can chat.'

When I came back through to the lounge, I could see that Joan had laid pieces of paper out on the coffee table.

'You've been busy,' I said.

'Yes. Just a little. It's a meal rota for Primrose. Would you add your name, Rita?'

'Of course. Just tell me where.'

'I wondered if you could be Thursday?' Julie's doing Monday, lasagne. I'm Tuesday, casserole, beef. Wednesday's Beattie, sausage surprise, Friday's a fish and chip supper provided by… Justine, Saturday…' 'Just a minute Joan. When you say Justine do you mean Justine Smart from Boughden Hall?'

'The self-same person,' she smiled.

'But she's not cul de sac.'

'No, but Bill is and you know he's seeing quite a lot of her.'

'Yes. That had rather come to my attention.'

'Justine said that she'd very much like to be part of our group and help. I thought… well… well actually Rita everyone else has been all right with it. Rita, will you be Thursday?'

'Yes. What's Thursday?'

'Jacket potato and mince in gravy, or as an option tuna in mayo.'

'I'll do it. I must say it's strange though what's happening in this cul de sac. Outsiders getting onto rotas.'

'Rita. Calm down.'

'I'm sorry Joan. I didn't mean to snap but I'm feeling under a lot of stress lately.'

'I know. And you've had Sid's little illness to add to everything else.'

'You're right, of course Joan but I don't think we should categorise illnesses. You're either ill or you're not. The illness might be minor but if you're unwell it's a big thing for you.'

'I stand chastised,' Joan said.

'How will I know Primrose's choice for the jacket potato?'

'She'll push a note through your door Thursday morning between 9-11a.m., before she goes off to work.'

'I'll just put a note on my kitchen planner. Help yourself to more coffee Joan, there's plenty in the pot.'

When I returned Joan said, 'I've put a rota together for the men to help with the garden at Primrose and Brian's. I'll not ask Sid to be part of it, not at the moment.'

'He's quite well now, as long as he takes his time and doesn't rush. I'm sure he could do something that didn't cause too much exertion.'

'No. I wouldn't dream of asking. There are enough men to help anyway.'

I felt sad and useless again, only now I was feeling it for Sid as well. I felt as though we were being excluded from cul de sac activities. I didn't say anything.

Joan finished her coffee and went back

home. I sat and thought about my new venture. The venture only Justine Smart knew anything about. The new venture I was oh, so excited about. My new post as volunteer guide at Boughden Hall.

I'd filled in all the forms and had a short interview. And now, after the acceptance came a letter inviting me to attend the welcome talk for new volunteers and also to do a 'mini-shift' the following Thursday. I was thrilled and it was the lift I needed after my low spell of the last few weeks.

Despite my best efforts, I hadn't actually mentioned any of this to Sid. I would do it tonight. I felt sure he would be thrilled for me.

I waited until after supper. Sid was surprised but he also said that he was sure that if that was what I wanted I'd probably be one of the best room stewards they'd ever seen at Boughden Hall. He doesn't say much, Sid, but sometimes he does get it 'just right'.

After that it was phone time, landline of course. I called everyone in the cul de sac and told them my news. Just chatting about the new venture

with my neighbours and friends really lifted my
spirits. If we'd have had stairs in our bungalow
I'd definitely have gone up them with a spring
in my step.

A BOUGHDEN VOLUNTEER

My slot was 1-4p.m. on Thursday afternoon. Sid waved me off at the door. He was thrilled for me and promised to visit the hall on one of my Thursdays when I was 'bedded in', so that he could see me in situ.

I allowed myself 45 minutes for the journey just in case there were any delays. There weren't. I was there at 12.30p.m.. I took myself across to the café to kill time.

As I turned to sit down with my drink I saw Justine sitting at one of the tables. She motioned me to join her. I went across and sat down. 'I'm early,' I said. 'I allowed extra time for traffic.'

'It might be when you've finished the traffic builds up, when everyone is leaving the hall. I hope Sid's in charge of the cooking tonight.' She smiled.

'I've left him instructions,' I said. Which was true, I had. The potatoes for us and Primrose were washed and left with instructions for cooking in the microwave. One of the machines better uses, I think. We would be having tuna as that was Primrose's choice and as I didn't want Sid to feel lost in his culinary duties, I thought it best to just go with one option.

'Looking forward to this afternoon?' Justine asked.

'I am. I've always wanted to be a volunteer at a house such as Boughden.

'That's good. Enthusiasm is always ninety-nine per cent of the job when you're a volunteer. You'll be with me first for a short lecture about how we work around the hall and then you'll go under the wing of one of our experienced room stewards. I'm sure you'll soon get to know the ropes. It's all quite straightforward.'

'How many of us are starting this afternoon?'

'Just three of you.'

'Oh, quite a small group then?'

'Yes, but three or four new volunteers is quite enough to manage at one time.' Justine smiled and looked at her watch. 'It's ten to,' she said, 'I'd better get along but you finish your drink Rita. I'll see you in the reception at 1p.m..

I did as I was told. I felt ever so slightly chastised by Justine even though I suppose she hadn't said anything in the slightest way to upset me. I suppose it was just her manner. Brusque, that was the word for her, brusque. I finished my drink and made sure I was at the reception area with a couple of minutes to spare. As I stood waiting for the other volunteers and Justine to appear I wondered if it was Justine's organisational skills and manner that had been the attraction for Bill?

The other volunteers appeared and we introduced ourselves to each other. We wouldn't always be at the hall together on a Thursday. Well, I would but the other volunteers both had different days. This was just a 'get to know the hall' event set up for us 'newbies'.

The clock in the reception struck one and before its chime had finished Justine entered the reception from her office. On the dot.

'Ah ladies, hello,' she said. 'I assume you've all introduced yourselves?'

We all nodded and smiled in unison.

'Well, follow me and we'll go through to my office.'

Justine ushered me into her office as if we were old school chums. I don't know if I liked her familiarity. Today just seemed to be not quite right. Perhaps it was me. I'm sure I would be all right once we got going properly with the job in hand.

'Ladies,' Justine enthused as we stood in the office, 'please, take a seat. We don't stand on ceremony here.' We all sat down and undid coats and fiddled with handbags. I could sense Justine watching us, keeping us under scrutiny.

'Now, I suppose we should start. Daphne, Glenis and Rita, I'm pleased on behalf of Boughden Hall to welcome you as volunteers and I truly hope you'll enjoy volunteering with us.' Justine began. And then she looked at us. I felt old at the side of Daphne and Glenis. Daphne didn't look younger but she acted younger and she had a keen glint in her eye. Glenis looked similar to me in age and dress sense but even she had a tattoo. A discreet one just below her left thumb knuckle. I noticed it when she removed her glove. It was a yellow rose, the stem continuing down towards her wrist. I thought it looked beautiful. Now I felt old. Very old. What on earth was I doing here? Perhaps I should give up now and return to the relative safety of the cul de sac.

Justine continued and told us about the history of the hall and then went onto what would be expected of us. It was all pretty straightforward stuff really. And Daphne and Glenis were easy to get on with. They obviously knew each other before volunteering at the hall. I was on my own. What did I want? I wanted to be a volunteer! There and then I decided that I had come on this journey and I would make a go of it. It was something I had thought of doing and now *I* would do it.

After all the chat Justine said there would be a short film. It would say more about the history of the hall and about the way we, as volunteers, were to behave with members of the public who were visiting the hall and the correct etiquette should we bump into a Boughden. Not to speak and avoid eye contact seemed to be de rigueur re the Boughdens.

Then surprise, surprise, tea and a cream slice from the Boughden Hall tea room. At this point Justine left us for about twenty minutes but it meant that Daphne, Glenis and myself had time to chat. *Bonding time*, Justine had called it. Apparently, it was something the hall liked all the volunteers to do. When   Justine returned she said that it was now time to move on and spend some time with experienced volunteers. I would be with Gordon in the Solar, upstairs. Daphne was in the Great Hall with Judith, (Judith appeared quite stern but I assumed her 'nice' side would appear). Glenis was with Nick in the Library. Suddenly it was becoming like a giant, living game of Cluedo. I was enjoying every minute of it. The time with our mentors passed far too quickly. Justine came and gathered us together and then it was back to her office.

'Well, ladies, how's it been?'

'Wonderful,' we chimed in unison.

'Good. That's good to hear,' Justine replied, then, 'well, intro session over. The next time you come you'll go straight to your appointed rooms on the days and times given to you in your letters of introduction to the hall. Your mentors will be there waiting for you, and, that's when the real work begins. So ladies, Boughden Hall looks forward to seeing you all next week. Goodbye.'

We said our goodbyes to Justine and each other and left. I felt exhilarated. I couldn't wait to get home and tell Sid all my news.

Sid had set the table and everything was waiting for me. I was amazed at the trouble he'd gone to. There was even a posy of flowers on the table. 'I thought you might appreciate them,' he said, 'after all you have been with the upper crust this afternoon. They must have floral arrangements every time they dine.'

'I expect so,' I said, as we sat down for our meal. 'Have you taken Primrose's round yet?' I asked. 'Yes. Just before you came in. My timing was perfect. I watched for her coming back from the hospital.'

'Good idea. She'll be off back again in

an hour or two.'

'Daresay. Anyway, let's not let ours go cold.'

Over dinner I told Sid how everything had gone at the hall.

'You've had a good afternoon then?'

'Yes. I have. I can't wait until next time.'

On her way out to the hospital Primrose called round to return the plate and the dish. 'There was no need to come now,' I said, 'it would have waited.'

'I know, but I wanted to, and to say thank you to you both, and to Sid, for the posy of flowers. Thank you. It was very thoughtful.'

I knew from her stance that something wasn't quite right. 'What is it Primrose. What's the matter?' 'Brian,' she said, 'it's Brian. They've called me to go back to the hospital. Could you come with me Rita?'

'Of course. I'll just get my coat.'

Primrose talked all the way to the hospital. I let her carry on. I didn't interrupt or add comment.

It was only a ten-minute drive although it seemed to take forever. All the traffic lights were against us.

Primrose seemed much brighter and had calmed down a little by the time we had reached our destination. It was a relief to me although I knew there would be a bigger challenge facing us. Hospitals don't usually call you for nothing.

I went up to the ward with Primrose. 'I'll wait here, in the corridor,' I pointed to some chairs. I'll be there, where the seats are and if you need me just come for me. Is that all right?'

'Yes. Just knowing I'm not on my own is a great relief.'

I seemed to be in the corridor for an age but each time I checked my watch time was only another five minutes further on. I hoped that all was well but you can never be certain. *Hospitals are funny places*, I thought, *filled in equal measure with feelings of happiness and relief or abject sorrow.*

It was Thursday evening. I wondered about Sid. It was coming up to nine o'clock. He was probably making a drink and getting ready for Death in Paradise. It was one of our favourites. And contrary to my first thoughts the young priest from Father Ted now filled the role of Police Inspector Jack Mooney. And filled it very well, I thought. You always wonder with these things when there's a cast change but this one was all right. It had my seal of approval.

I wondered if there were any magazines around but a glance up and down the corridor told me not. I checked my watch again, it had just turned nine o'clock. Sid would be taking the lid off the biscuit barrel. That done, he would look thoughtfully at the contents before coming to a decision and then he would prepare to dunk the biscuit of his choice into his mug of cocoa. He was very predictable was Sid.   I heard the door to the ward open and close. I glanced across. A young nurse approached.

'Your friend Primrose was getting worried about you, she said you'd been here for quite a while and as I was preparing the supper drinks she asked that I might offer you a drink. Would you like some Horlicks?'

'If it's not too much trouble,' I replied, 'that would be lovely.'

'I won't be a minute. I'll just finish taking the drinks round the ward and then I'll be out to you.'

'Thank you. Can I just ask, how is Brian?' I don't know what I expected her to say but her reply was the usual, 'he's comfortable', and then she went back through to the ward.

When Primrose eventually returned, I was just finishing my drink. I hadn't had Horlicks for years. *I must get some*, I thought. *It was quite delicious.* It made me think of an uncle of mine. He swore by it for getting a good night's sleep.

'Was that good?' Primrose asked.

'Excellent. Took me back to past times. Memories are wonderful things, aren't they?'

'Yes,' Primrose replied.

'How's Brian? I asked the nurse but she would only say that he was comfortable.'

'They have pat lines and phrases I think, but she was right, he does seem comfortable. He was out of it for a while but then he's been bright as anything for the past ten minutes. We chatted about a lot of things. He's already planning for Open Gardens Day.'

'Oh, that's good. I bet Frank will be interested to know that.'

'I expect so. Anyway, it looks like I'll be here a while longer and it's coming up to quarter to ten and Brian's asleep again now so I could drop you home.'

'No. Don't be silly. If I'm going home Sid can come for me but I'll leave it up to you, you say whether you want me to stay or not.'

'I'd love you to stay but that would be imposing and I won't do that. Could you phone Sid and ask him to come for you?'

'I will do.' I stood up. 'Could you take this mug back onto the ward for me? And then I'll pop my head round the ward door to let the desk nurse know when I've left. I won't disturb you, and Primrose, if you want anything, just pick up the phone and ask. You'll do that won't you?'

Primrose smiled. I gave her a hug. It's not the type of thing we do, we cul de sac-ers, but just now it seemed appropriate.

TO THE HALL

Gordon met me at reception the following Thursday when I was due at Boughden Hall. We walked to the Solar together and chatted along the way.

Gordon was extolling the virtues of Justine Smart. *How extraordinary* I thought; she can wrap the menfolk around her little finger.

When we started our stint on duty Gordon gave me the once over; making sure that I was wearing the correct 'navy' for a room steward. I had been provided with a red and white polka dot neckerchief and name badge at the induction the previous week.

'Perfect, Rita,' Gordon said and smiled, perhaps a little too enthusiastically.

I had room guides to give out as and when visitors came into the Solar *but* (apart from a 'good afternoon') I must only respond verbally if a question or remark was made directly to me. This had been hammered home to me last week by Justine. 'Visitors,' she had said, 'do not like to be hassled by over-enthusiastic volunteers. We would like them to return, *not,* I repeat *not,* run for the hills.'

I could hear Justine's voice in my head. It was as if she were there.

Gordon allowed me to have the first four or five visitors. After that we went in turn. He was pleased he said with my progress. Now it was my turn to smile. And I did. Flattery does, if nothing else, brighten the world a little.

At 2.45p.m. it was my time for a fifteen-minute break. And welcome it was. I headed to the staff room. It was located just behind the café. Tea or coffee was provided free of charge, and a biscuit. Cake was a different matter. I had tea and a chocolate Hob Nob. Bliss. I wondered about Primrose. Without her I wouldn't have been here as a volunteer at Boughden. After all she was the driving force; the one who had organised the trip. *Yes*, I thought, *without her I wouldn't be here and Bill wouldn't have met Justine.* It made me feel slightly sad. To think of what had come from our cul de sac visit to Boughden and now Primrose fixed as she was to Brian's bedside at the hospital. I brought myself back to the present, finished my drink and washed my cup. Then I went and re-joined Gordon in the Solar.

'We've had quite a flurry through,' he said. 'It might be quietish now for you while I have my break. Do you think you'll be able to manage? If you get stuck just press button 3 on the intercom. You'll get an immediate response.'

'I'm sure I shall be all right,' I said.

'That's the ticket,' Gordon replied. 'I'll see you in fifteen.'

And he was off. *See you in fifteen.* He's making out he's trendy, I thought. Well, if it pleases him, I smiled to myself.

I was hoping I'd have a flurry of people through, like Gordon, but I didn't. I suppose because the hall closed at four o'clock you wouldn't get many in for the last hour. After all, who'd want to pay to visit somewhere for that amount of time. You wouldn't have time to go round the grounds or visit the café. And believe me, the latter is a definite 'must do' whenever Sid and I are out on a visit anywhere.

When Gordon returned, I'd nothing of interest to report, but he had.

'I think I saw a friend of yours in the café with Justine as I was coming back into the hall,' he said, 'is it Bill?'

'I have a neighbour called Bill, 'I said, 'and he's also a friend. How do you know it's him?'

'From your visit to the hall earlier in the year. I was on room duty. And, I have a good memory for faces.'

'Oh,' I said.

Gordon continued, 'And I heard Justine

call him Bill. It made me do a double take. It's the Bill you know. I'm certain.'

'I suppose it might be,' I said.

'Mmm,' he said, a glint in his eye, 'they seemed to be getting quite pally.'

Sid couldn't understand my humour when I returned home. I didn't want to be tittle-tattling. It wasn't my way but he drew it out of me. 'I'm not sure I'm keen on Gordon. He's my mentor for a few weeks at the hall, until I'm properly bedded in.'

'Is that all?' he said.

I looked at him. Sometimes Sid just didn't understand.

'Oh, by the way,' he said, 'there's a meeting tomorrow night, seven o'clock, Bill's conservatory.'

BILL'S HEADS UP

'Did he say he'd have agendas ready?' I asked Sid.

'Not sure. He just said could we all be there and prompt.'

'He's changed since he started walking out with Justine. I don't think he knows quite where he is sometimes. What about refreshments? Will he want myself and Beattie on that? Only we've no Thin Arrowroot.'

'I'm sure we'll manage,' Sid said, and then added, 'anyway, I'm off in a minute or two. It's Men in Sheds, so if you need me, you'd best get me on my mobile.'

'Just a minute Sid, before you go. Who's going to Men in Sheds, will Bill be there?'

'No.'

'No?'

'Yes, that's what he said. He's busy this morning.'

'Busy at what, did he say?'

'No, and before you ask I wasn't going to fish for any details.'

'Oh, well if you think on bring a packet of Thin Arrowroot back with you. And what are you making today, anything special?

'I'm doing poker work name plates,

you know the type of thing, the ones children have on their bedroom doors. They'll have a child's name on, and I'll do the odd one with 'Keep Out', and 'No Grown Ups,' but names are my main stock in trade. I've done some for boys, and girls, of course. I've a few here, if you want to have a look.'

Sid took some of the wooden name plates from his bag. They looked very professional, and I told him so. I read aloud, *Cody's Room, Charlie's Room, Archie's Room*. 'I haven't seen any girls' names, Sid. Where are they?' Sid opened another bag, 'Here,' he said, '*Sophie's Room*'.

'That's lovely. Some little girl will be pleased to have that on her bedroom door.'

'Yes. Well as I said, we're very twenty-first century at Men in Sheds. And we also do some for adults, you know the sort of thing, *Mum's Kitchen, Friends always* .... Oh and you'll like this one our Rita, *The Man Cave*. You know, it's for a man to put on his shed, or cave, I suppose…'

For someone who usually didn't say much Sid was on a roll. 'All right I get the idea. Are these name plates for something special. I mean have you anywhere in mind for them. A local shop or something?'

'No. Although I want to ask Bill tonight

if we can sell them at the Open Gardens event.'

'Mmm.'

'All right love, I'd best get off.'

And he was gone.

I telephoned Beattie. She hadn't heard from Bill. It made me wonder about the rest of the cul de sac. I checked. There was only Beattie not heard so I thought perhaps Ray had forgotten to mention it. I phoned Beattie back. I was correct, but that made me wonder why Ray hadn't gone to Men in Sheds. I could hear him coughing every now and again in the background. It wasn't, in my opinion bad enough to keep someone away from a hobby, so I asked.

'He's just a bit off colour,' Beattie said. She didn't go on to give any more details so I didn't ask.

'Will he be all right for tonight, at Bill's?'

'I should think so,' Beattie replied.

'Oh, only we don't want him passing things round the cul de sac, not with Brian being ill.'

'Well Brian and Primrose won't be there. They'll be apologies for absence.'

'Yes, but even so, you have to be careful.'
'We'll both be there, me and Ray. Oh, and by the way Rita, I've bought a packet of Thin Arrowroot.'
'Good. I was wondering about that. I asked Sid to bring a packet if he thought on, but it doesn't matter. It's the belt and braces approach to things that I like, as you know.'
'Yes. All right Rita, bye and see you tonight.'

I was left pretty much twiddling my thumbs. I wondered what to do. Baking always made me feel better if I was a bit down. And I was. It was because I was wondering what would happen at the meeting tonight. I had misgivings about it for some reason.   I went into the kitchen and set about making a treacle tart. One of Sid's favourites. It would be ready when he returned from Men in Sheds.

Being in the kitchen certainly lifted my mood. Not only did I make the treacle tart I also made other pastry offerings; pasties, meat and cheese, jam tarts, (using up the remains of the apricot, damson and strawberry jams in my cupboard) I felt I'd had a very productive morning.

Just before 1 o'clock I heard Sid come round the side of the house. He opened the back door,

'Mmm, something smells good. Have you been baking love?'

'Yes, and one of your favourites.' I drew the tea towel covering from the freshly baked treacle tart. 'Treacle tart,' Sid said, 'wonderful.' I noticed Sid had a bag of something in his hand. He put it down as he took his coat off.

'What's in there, then? I asked.

'It's the door name plates I showed this morning. I've added a few more and thought I'd bring a few samples across to show to Bill at the meeting tonight.'

I started to set the table for lunch.

At 6.30p.m. Sid and I set off for Bill's house for the meeting. Once inside it was obvious we were all there apart of course from Brian and Primrose.

'Are the agendas ready?' I asked Bill.

'I've put them on the seats in the conservatory. I think I've an addition for any other business,' Sid said, holding up his carrier bag.

'What is it?' Bill asked.

'Name plates made from wood,' Sid replied. Bill just managed a muffled 'oh', and a puzzled look.

I left Sid and went through to the kitchen where Beattie was setting up trays for the drinks later on. 'Do you need a hand?' I asked.

'No. I've put all the cups and saucers out and we can do the biscuits later.' Beattie held up a packet of Thin Arrowroot.

'Are the kettles filled?' I asked.

'Yes, all done.'

'I'll go and join Sid then.'

Beattie suddenly looked concerned. 'Rita, are you all right? I mean you seem a little distracted.'

'I've something hanging over me. It's, well, well don't think I'm being silly but I've a strange sense of foreboding about tonight.'

I think I took Beattie by surprise. She didn't say anything and I left her where she was.

By 6.55p.m. we were all, except for Bill, sitting and waiting in the conservatory. I was sure I could hear Bill on the phone, but didn't comment. He came through and joined us all a couple of minutes later. I knew he'd be in the conservatory before seven o'clock. As I've mentioned before, he's very precise. Runs things with military precision and planning. That's why the cancelling of committee meetings at such short notice was so strange and so unlike him. Anyway, not so tonight. 'Good to have everyone here and on time,' Bill said, 'right we'll get straight on with the meeting. Are there any apologies for absence?'

'Only Primrose and Brian,' I said, 'which of course is understandable.'

'Quite, quite,' Bill replied, 'and to that we must also add our PCSO, more on that later.'

The agenda was all the usual stuff really. The rota for Brian and Primrose's garden and help with meals. The visit to Boughden Hall and how well it had been received was discussed and then we came to 'what next'? It was decided to leave 'what next' until the next committee meeting. Bill then said that he had received an email from the local constabulary. Our PCSO wouldn't be able to attend the meeting tonight and a crime report for our area was included as an attachment. He said he had printed copies off for us and they were attached to the agendas.

We all knew there had been nothing re crime to report in the cul de sac but it was always interesting to hear what was happening locally. We felt that keeping abreast of any situation made us more alert and so helped prevent us from falling into the local crime statistics.

Not since the Cliff Richard cds/car incident had there been any mentionable crime in the cul de sac. Thankfully for us there had been only two crimes in the area in the past month. We were all relieved at that and then Bill announced the local crime detail. Both quite minor but bothersome nonetheless if they affected you. They were, a case of littering on Bulldog Lane and the theft of a bicycle from the primary school. Bill continued, 'Investigations were ongoing into the incident of the stolen bicycle and a litter team had been sent urgently to tackle the problem on Bulldog Lane. Now, moving on, we need to think about our Open Gardens Day. Summer will soon be with us, the lighter nights fast approaching. Are we all going to be ready? Can I rely on you all again?' 'You can rely on me,' Frank said. 'I'm already making plans. I fancy doing some really large hanging baskets. They'll be three or four foot in diameter. And tubes, lots of hanging tubes, three or four foot long and twelve or eighteen inch in diameter. What do you think?'

'Go for it Frank,' Fred replied. 'I'll have to see what I can come up with.'

'Joan said, 'I thought you were doing a model of a bowling green complete with three crowns.'

'Shh,' Fred replied. 'That's my little secret.' And then he whistled, quietly to himself.

'Well, it certainly seems that everyone has plenty of ideas. I think that means we're on. We'll get diaries out now and plump shall we for our Open Gardens weekend? How does the weekend of 13th/14th July sound?'

Everyone agreed, it was voted in and we carried on. Bill continued, 'Now, any other business, because I have something, now what time do we have?' He looked at his watch, 'Seven forty-five.' Now fifteen minutes and then we'll be done. Yes, that works.'

We all looked at Bill. He seemed to be going all strange, suddenly. I nudged Sid, 'Better get your AOB in now,' I whispered.

Bill looked at me. 'Now Rita, you know

we don't like whispering. If there's anything to say, we'd all like to hear. It is a committee meeting.'

I felt myself colour. Sid spoke up. 'Rita was just reminding me.' He held up his bag.

'These are wooden nameplates for children's rooms, and others. We do a few designs at Men in Sheds, and as you know Bill any name can be added.' Sid took one of the name plates from his bag. 'Pass it round so you can all see. We, the men at Men in Sheds, wondered if they could be sold at the Open Gardens Day as a fundraiser. We thought it might go to the hospital where Brian is, seeing as he is one of the Men in Sheds.'

There were murmurings of 'good idea', 'how much,' 'can folk place orders?'

The committee decided in favour. Sid smiled. I could see he was pleased.   These nameplates were his 'baby' at the moment and although half of the committee attended Men in Sheds , rules have to be adhered to. After all, a committee is a committee.   Bill looked at his watch. It was five to eight. 'Well, I think that concludes things. I'll draw the meeting to a close.'

'But we haven't had your Any Other Business,' Joan remarked.

'It's not eight o'clock yet,' Bill replied.

There was noise in the kitchen. Beattie and I turned. 'We'll go and make the drinks,' Beattie said.

'No,' Bill said, 'it's all right. I'll go.'

Everyone in the conservatory was slightly stunned by Bill's actions but we remained seated in the conservatory.

Only a matter of minutes later he came back through carrying a tray loaded with champagne flutes all bubbles and fizz. By his side was Justine Smart, all smiles, as was Bill. Bill looked at her and then at us. 'Come on everyone, take a glass and drink to us. Justine and I are engaged.'

The glasses were passed round and there was a toast to the happy couple.

Justine held up her left hand to show off a princess cut diamond solitaire. Bill leant across and kissed her.

A ROYAL CELEBRATION

'That was a surprise wasn't it?' I said to Joan the next time we were volunteering at the charity shop.

'The engagement?' she questioned.

'Yes, the engagement.'

'I thought you'd have seen it coming. You're usually onto things of a romantic persuasion.'

'Well, I didn't see this. But it's good to have something good to celebrate. We've spent the last few months worrying about Brian and Primrose.'

'Yes,' Joan said, 'but he's doing all right now and should be home soon if Primrose's predictions come true.'

Just then Muriel came out from the office. 'Ladies, I've just had Primrose on the phone. The hospital are delighted with the amount raised for the ward at our little event. They're going to organise a little 'do' at the hospital and have a proper hand over. They've asked the local paper to come along to take photos. And ladies, could you reprise your gypsy costumes and don't forget the crystal ball.'

Joan and I looked at each other and laughed. 'We'd better go and raid the clothes rails again, if that's all right,' I said.

'Of course,' Muriel replied, and then she went back into her office.

'Isn't that wonderful news?' Joan said.

'Yes,' I answered, 'and there'll be more cash to follow later after the Open Gardens and the help from Men in Sheds.'

'And Brian might just be home for that,' Joan added.

'I'm pleased that everything seems to be turning out all right. And Brian loves his garden. Perhaps we'll have a wonderful summer to look forward to if everything keeps on track.'

Suddenly, the office door was flung open in such a rush that it quite startled Joan and I. It was Muriel again. 'This is hot off the press ladies. We have a new member of the Royal Family. Meghan of Sussex has had a baby. It's a boy, 7lb 3oz and as yet, unnamed.

Joan and I cheered. 'You know what this means?' I said.

'Yes,' Joan replied, 'a cul de sac party with tea and China cups, sandwiches and lots of cake. When we've finished here we'd best get home; discuss and organise.'

A few days after his birth the royal family announced that the new addition to the family would be named,

Archie Harrison Mountbatten-Windsor.

He was born on the 6th May 2019

Rita's recipe for Treacle Tart,

(one of Sid's favourites)

Set the oven to 230c, Gas mark 8, A hot oven. Temperatures are a guide only, check your own oven settings.

6'' - 7'' flan dish.

Ingredients

For the pastry;
4oz, 115g plain flour
2oz, 58g margarine
1-2 tablespoons cold water

For the filling;
6oz, 170g golden syrup
50z, 144g fine breadcrumbs (white)
Grated rind and juice of 1 medium lemon

Method

In a mixing bowl put the plain flour, to this add the margarine, broken into small pieces. Combine mixture rubbing through fingertips until a breadcrumb-like consistency is reached. When the breadcrumb stage is reached, add the water a little at a time and mix well with a fork. When the mixture starts to form a ball, mix together with hands. You may add a little more water if required. Leave pastry to rest in the fridge until required.
In a basin, grate the rind of the lemon and to this add the juice, the breadcrumbs and the golden syrup. Mix well until all the ingredients are combined.

Take pastry from fridge, roll out and line the flan dish with the pastry. Prick the base of the tart a few times with a fork. Keep any trimmings of pastry to decorate the top of the tart.

To the pastry dish add the treacle mixture. If you have pastry trimmings, twist them and place in a lattice fashion across the treacle mixture. Bake in the oven for 20 or 30 minutes, until the pastry is cooked through.

**The treacle mixture will rise slightly when
cooked.**
This tart can be served hot or cold.

ABOUT THE AUTHOR

Margaret Holbrook grew up in Cheshire where she still lives. Her work has been published in anthologies and magazines and broadcast on radio.

She writes fiction, plays and poetry.

In 2014, her play *The Supper Party,* was a finalist in the 'Grand Words' competition run in conjunction with the *Grand Theatre,* Blackpool.

Her short story, *Our Brian,* was longlisted for the BBC Radio 4 programme, 'Opening Lines' in the same year.

In 2015, her play *Sandy's Ashes* was performed at Congleton Festival and in November 2015 her short story *Pig Man* was shortlisted for the Cheshire Prize for Literature and is published in the Cheshire Prize Anthology, *Patches of Light.*

In May 2019, her play *The Bus Stop* had its first performance at The Old Saw Mill, Congleton.

Website:

https://mgth13.wixsite.com/margaretholbrook

Follow on facebook:

www.facebook.com/margaretholbrookauthor

And, if you would be kind enough to leave a review or rating you can do this on Amazon, goodreads or any bookshop website.

Thank You

www.ingramcontent.com/pod-product-compliance
Lightning Source LLC
Chambersburg PA
CBHW051813050726

47598CB00006B/2546